Requiem

Requiem
Poems of the Terezín Ghetto

PAUL B. JANECZKO

CANDLEWICK PRESS

First paperback edition 2013

The Library of Congress has cataloged the hardcover edition as follows:

Janeczko, Paul B.
Requiem : poems of the Terezín ghetto / Paul B. Janeczko. — 1st ed.
p. cm.
ISBN 978-0-7636-4727-8 (hardcover)
1. Theresienstadt (Concentration camp) — Juvenile poetry.
2. Children's poetry, American.
I. Title. II. Title: Poems of the Terezín ghetto.
PS3560.A465R47 2011
811'.54 — dc22   2010038882

ISBN 978-0-7636-6465-7 (paperback)

13 14 15 16 17 18 BVG 10 9 8 7 6 5 4 3 2 1

Printed in Berryville, VA, U.S.A.

This book was typeset in Dante.

Candlewick Press
99 Dover Street
Somerville, Massachusetts 02144

visit us at www.candlewick.com

For Liz,
guide, fan, dear and constant friend
&

in memory of Jedd Bowers (1975 – 2009)
Rest, O kind and gentle soul

Contents

Margit Zadok / 13597

Papa didn't move.
He stood in the street
still as a lamppost
eyes locked on the nightmare
that had been his shop.
Windows smashed,
scattered glass winking in the sun,
the bottom half of his sign
Rosenberg's Fine Linens of Prague
blackened, burned.
Delicate handkerchiefs
now fallen white leaves.
Papa bowed his head
in prayer
or in despair—
I couldn't tell.
A white linen tablecloth

edged with pink roses —
Mama's favorite pattern —
flowed like a bride's train
from sidewalk to curb to gutter.
Papa stared at black boot marks
crossing it like sins.
A man and a woman walked from the shop
arms filled with linens.
"You!" Papa shouted.
"You cannot steal from me!"
The woman looked away.
The man smiled at Papa's rage.
"Know your place, Jew," the man snarled.
"Know your place."
As they walked off,
a napkin dropped from the woman's arms
falling to the ground
as noiselessly as snow.

Victor Cizik / 23790

Snow was in the air
as we marched from the station
that November afternoon
as solemn as the sky,
three hundred volunteers
packed into Transport Ca-114 from Prague
to ready the fortress
for those who would follow
to this place Hitler gave to the Jews.
The Nazis watched
as we measured, sawed planks for bunks
three high, sometimes four,
painted and plastered one barracks then another—
Magdeburg, Dresden, Hanover, Hamburg—
all with good German names.

We knew others would come to this place,
family, neighbors, strangers
to this place Hitler gave to the Jews
this "haven for the elderly."
The Nazis told us
that our work would help protect us
and others we knew who would be arriving.
So we sawed, painted, hammered.

The Nazi promises proved to be nothing
when names appeared on the transport lists
first in summer
again when snow was on the ground
as they marched to the station
climbed into cattle cars
that trembled
as the impatient locomotive
dragged them into the dark
of no more promises.

I am Miklos.

The younger boys in L410

call me Professor.

Because I know many words?

Because of my large glasses?

Because I like to write

in a small notebook

that I conceal from the guards

in my shoe?

I am fragile

with fear.

Marie Jelinek / 17789

The doors of the cattle car rumbled,
opened.
We spilled
onto the platform,
eager even for snow and wind.
We found floodlights
barking dogs
vile shouts from SS soldiers.
Shoves and commands—
"Line up!
Hurry!" —
were met with screams
crying
names called in darkness.
Crammed through the *Schleuse,*
where papers were issued
and most of our belongings

stolen, replaced with promises.

Beasts of burden,

we shouldered bundles

of what pieces of the past

we were allowed to keep

as we joined the river of fear,

a current of shuffling feet, sobs, and whimpers

that crept past dark mouths

of archways and windows

to Terezín.

Erich Rosenberg / 43458

Bedbugs are not the amiable creatures
of nursery rhymes,
my lecture began.
Far from it.
Filled with blood
they are the size of an apple seed.
Unless engorged
they can move with the speed of an ant.
You will note
that their bites are often in clusters
or in a line of three —
breakfast, lunch, and dinner,
as they say —
although they feast only
in the last hours of night.

Each female can lay five eggs each day —
tiny, as you might imagine,

the color and size of a grain or two of salt—
but they hatch in two weeks.
We will never be rid of them.

They hide in tiny places—
cracks in the wall or floor
under your mattress
in your mattress—
until it is time to crawl over you.
Drawn by your warmth,
your breath,
they find a spot to suck your blood
injecting their saliva
leaving a blister, a rash
that must *not* be scratched.
That will bring passing relief
but blood as well
more blood
on bedclothes, sheets,
under fingernails.
You must resist.
You must endure.

I see
Old Man Asher
a skeleton
holding a stick
thicker than his arm
to keep away the rats.

Tomasz Kassewitz / 11850

For nearly sixteen years of Fridays
Willi and I played chess in the park
unless snow drove us
to the back corner of Bloom's.
Only for death—
when my beloved Helen passed,
when his son fell through the ice—
did we miss.
Willi brought a small brown paper bag
of white peppermints.
I hid two cigars
in my shirt pocket until later.
Two warriors, we said little
as move led to countermove.
Later, board and pieces put away,
cigars lit,

we talked the talk of old men
warmed on the park bench.

On a most glorious morning in October
Willi placed the peppermints on the table
but did not sit.
I looked up at the face of sorrow.
He picked up the white king
then laid it softly on its side.
"I can no longer play with you,"
said a false voice.
The sun is blue
would have made as much sense.
"It is forbidden, my friend,
to *fraternize* with a Jew."
I looked at his king.
"I must go," he whispered.
"They are watching."

Only when my bones chilled
in the darkening day
did I stand

and with a single swipe
clear the table
of chessmen, peppermints,
and walk into the new night.

SS Captain Bruno Krueger

Two Jews tried to escape—
one old, one no more than a boy—
but dogs cornered them and
my guards dragged them back
to the far corner of the yard
for the lesson.

We herded all the Jew swine
close to the gallows
where the old Jew stood on the wagon
noosed.
I ordered my Jews closer.
Close enough to hear
the twig snap of his neck.
Close enough to smell
when he shit himself in death.
Close enough to see his face darken,

his tongue poke from his mouth.
There was crying when he swung,
some mumbled words
(hate? prayers?).

As he hung and finished his death dance,
a guard brought forth the other man.
Man? Was he old enough to shave?
No matter.
He will be a teacher,
playing his part in today's lesson.
He was, perhaps, saving other Jews
who dreamed of freedom.

Hands tied behind his back,
kneeling in the mud
he looked at me with defiance.
I enjoyed the chance to show him,
to show all,
the impracticality of defiance.
Another Jew fetched a bucket
filled with paving stones.
I selected a stone,
carefully,

looking for one with sharp corners.
I handed it to him.
"Throw it," I said, indicating the boy.
"Like in your Old Testament."
He refused. Of course.
"But you must," I told him,
and nodded to the gallows Jew.
So he did.
"Forgive me," he cried. "I am sorry."

Faces can tell so much.
Some are like books,
with many chapters.
The boy's face first told fear
then resignation
finally defiance.
Ah, but the face of the executioner
was sad,
so very sad,
quickly changing to anger—
my face told no stories—
and then his face spoke hate.
He threw the first stone,
hitting the boy in the temple,

knocking him on his face.

The man looked at me.

I shook my head

and handed him another stone.

I would not be cheated.

The lesson must continue.

He threw another stone.

Another.

A fourth.

Blinded by tears

the man missed his next throw.

Prodded by the barrel of a guard's rifle,

he threw one more.

The boy was dead,

a black stone buried in the back of his head.

"Bravo," I cried. "Bravo,"

then shooed him back to the other Jews.

"Remember this, Jews," I said,

a wave of my arm at the corpses.

"Remember."

Anna Teller / 12727

At first, our music was secret
forbidden
played in attics and cellars
subdued by fear of discovery.
The body of a piano —
found who knows where —
was lugged to the frigid attic
set on crates
where Klein tuned it
coaxed from it Mozart, Janáček —
hope
for all who heard.
Sheet music smuggled into the ghetto,
instruments, as well, in parts
to be assembled by candlelight,
memorized music
written down, taught.

Until the day our music
was permitted by the Nazis,
who wanted the world to see
the civilized and charming ghetto
Hitler gave the Jews.
The Free Time Administration
gave us instruments
paper for composition
time to practice.
Nazi gifts given freely
with smiles for the camera
that filmed our good fortune.

False hope
said those who spoke
of transports and rumors of gas.
You are making music
in the shadow of the gallows.
They were right, we knew,
but we played nonetheless
played as only the heartbroken can play
a final performance
for it was always a final performance
for some in the orchestra.

Ullmann, Krása, Haas to Auschwitz.

And young Klein, too, east

leaving only the sweet ache of a last sonata.

Magnolia blossoms riot
over the fence
of the home of the Kommandant.
What could they want
on this side?

David Epstein / 12275

I wish I could kill one of them.

One.

A small number, no?

I would need no help.

Want none.

I would want my face

to be the last thing he saw before he died.

My face.

As the blade finds its way between his ribs —

at that instance I'd want him to see my face.

He would not know me.

I did nothing to you, he would think.

What he did, he did to all of us.

He would not understand

punishment for doing his duty.

I would like his last blood-choked moment

to be confused

before I heaved him
onto a pile of bodies on the hearse,
his legs, shoeless, hanging over the side.
I would like to feed him my Sarah's ashes
one spoonful after another
without pause
until he could no longer breathe.
Then I would force more ashes into his nose.
Whatever he choked down or spit out
I would replace with more
of my Sarah's ashes.
When he died I would cram
more ashes down his throat.
Dead or not
he must taste my Sarah's ashes.

Perhaps I would do nothing to him.
Nothing but watch him descend
into the hell of typhus,
fevered, slow of pulse,
vomiting down the front of his shirt,
clutching his wrenching stomach,
surrounded by friends and family
who could do nothing to help

except listen to his rambles
except clean up diarrhea
hour after hour.

Yes,
I wish I could kill one of them.
One.
A small number, no?
I would need no help
to deliver justice.

SS Kommandant Manfred Brandt &
SS Sergeant Dieter Hoffmann

What is your report, Dieter?

                    The Jews are playing music.
                    In the attics. Basements.

Let them.

                    But it is forbidden.

Dieter, imagine that you are one of them.

                    I, a Jew!

Humor me.

                    Yes, *Kommandant*.

Suppose you have time to do what you love.
Play your piano. Violin.
Play Bach, Mozart, Mendelssohn.

I despise their music.

But imagine that you love music,
a gift you were born with.
Now you get a chance to play for friends.

Yes?

How would you feel?

I would feel like a Jew swine.

Of course,
but what would be on your mind?

I . . .

Think, Dieter. What would be on your mind?

Music.

Music. Of this you are certain?

                        I am certain, *Kommandant*.

You would not think of escape?

                        No.

Rebellion? Anarchy?

                        Just music.

So, let the Jews play their music, Dieter.
In fact, we will do what we can —
within reason, of course —
to assist.
                        Understood.

Because, Dieter, the day will come
for all of them
when there will be no more music.

                        Understood.

Hilda Bartos

This was a good town.
Quiet.
Isolated.
My family farmed,
raised goats for generations
before war arrived,
a menacing visitor
that took away my town
because its walls,
empty barracks
would be easy to guard.
They liked the railroad
so close in Bohušovice.
I know this from Jakub
a ready listener at the tavern.

At first, workers
came to repair and prepare

for the Jews from Prague
moving to this "ghetto for the old"
notable persons of high regard,
invalid heroes from the war.

At Christmastime the first of the Jews arrived,
an endless funeral procession
of fumbling ancients,
women with babes in arms,
children stooped with fatigue and fear,
men with hats pulled down
all bearing a yellow star on their coats.
Through our streets a pitiful parade
to the barracks.

More came to our town.
They walked the same streets as I
but with eyes downcast.
I made a habit
of carrying crusts of bread
or chunks of apples
in my coat pockets
for the children
when no one was looking.

More came to our town.
More left.
We saw them in hearses
in the darkening afternoon.
We saw them trudging
to the station at dawn.

More came to our town
until we received the Notice of Displacement.
For the "war effort,"
we needed to sacrifice our homes.
"Where will we go?" we asked.
From the *Kommandant* a shrug
and a warning
that impeding the Führer's historic vision
would not be tolerated.

So I pack
to go to a sister in Salzburg.
Jakub will drive me to the station.
My town is no longer mine.
Death is in the air
stinging like the bitter cold.
We follow a hearse

past the town square.

My cousin whispers

of the horrors that await the Jews.

"Worse than this?" I ask.

"Worse than starvation and disease?"

His solemn nod

strips hope from me.

I shiver.

Rachel's birthday gift:
a cardboard box
which became a bed for her doll
even after the morning she found
curled with her doll
a dead mouse.

Valtr Eisinger / 11956

My dearest Vera,
You did not expect this.
Neither did I. But
it has come.
I will be included in the next transport,
which will assemble
in the barracks on Sunday morning.
We will be gone on Tuesday.
The die has been cast.
I have calmly accepted
the inexorable call of our Jewish destiny.
It is my greatest wish
that you remain calm, too.
I bless fate again
that you are not with me,
that you are spared all this.

I say good-bye to you
in the firm conviction
that we shall meet again
as free people.
And then, my beloved Vera,
I shall realize the dream
I so often dream.

I shall always think of you.
Thoughts of you will be
my morning prayer when I get up,
my evening prayer when I go to bed.
Memories of you will be a balm
to whatever blows fate deals me.

Should it happen, my dearest Vera,
that I do not return,
I set you free
of any promise you made me.
I would only wish
that the one to whom you give your hand
should love you
at least somewhat the way I love you.

Stooped Zelenka
awakes before light
moves among the dead
preparing them for the hearse.
But, like a crow,
she scavenges
under the pillows of the dead,
taking what they will not need.

Helena Berg / 13376

I dream of hugs.
Plump hugs from Mama,
slow hugs
smelling of lavender.
And Papa's quick hugs,
almost-by-accident hugs
given with a whiff of tobacco.
Aunt Hilda's hugs
punctuated by squeaks and clucks,
excessive since Uncle Karl left.

I wake to rare hugs, hurried
hugs, fragile hugs,
hugs as brittle
as the winter twigs that snap
as we walk
with eyes down
afraid to look at anything
ahead.

Aaron Nantova / 10123

His friends pulled Aaron back
from the fourth-floor window.
He sobbed,
"I can take no more.
I must fly away."
They begged him,
"Have heart!
Our people must endure!"
His sobbing slowly stopped,
gave way to shame,
mumbled thanks
in the embrace of friends.

That night he listened
to no voice but
his own

and plunged
to the cobbled courtyard,
stars witnessing
his flight.

Ruth Posner / 14161

Darkness covered us.
The rain and the November chill
bit through coats old and worn
no attire for a march.

We received no explanation
only a command to march.
So we marched
all of us—
thirty thousand? forty?—
moving through the gate
into the countryside
kept in check
by guards with bayonets.

After marching hours into day
we halted in a large meadow

not far from the mountains.

Rumors spread like typhus.

Surely we were brought to this cratered field

to be machine-gunned in the rain.

No shots were fired.

Only orders:

    "Line up!"

    "Do not talk!"

    "Do not move!"

So we stood in rows to be counted.

A silver plane circled.

Were we to be bombed?

The guards walked between the rows

counting

lashing out with their walking sticks.

No food.

No drink

No toilet.

We stood in rows to be counted again.

The Jewish Elders counted.

The Czech *strażnik*s counted.

No agreement in tallies.

We were counted again

as the silver plane circled.

By late afternoon
children cried out for food.
In the cold rain people died,
mostly the old,
slipping silently to the ground,
or the sick,
giving out a small cry
falling from the grasp of a friend
into a final silence.
They were standing in line,
then not.

The afternoon and the rain continued
into the darkness.
We were counted again.
Crying.
Searching the darkness for a familiar face.
Children holding hands, friends forever.
We stood in the darkness
and were counted again.

Then a new command
like a thunderclap:
    "Clear the valley!"

"Immediately!"
Then the crush of people
who wanted only the misery of prison.
The weak, the sick, the small fell.
To the delight of the guards,
many were lost under the wave.

The dead, the fallen,
were lifted by weak arms
and carried for hours
back to the ghetto
as the rain became mist,
the road endless.

The hearse
moves
slowly
like death itself.
We don't look.
We cannot bear
to see ourselves.

Sara Engel / 37124

I was lucky,
I was told,
to work indoors
in the bundles room,
small and airless,
two barred windows near the ceiling.
Three girls looked up when I walked in.
Two mumbled their names,
the third looked down.
Each had a bundle opened
on the floor before her,
like chaotic picnics.

Other bundles were piled along a wall,
each different.
One wrapped in a yellow-and-blue bedspread.
A white tablecloth, ringed with red tulips.

A child's pink blanket,
small with a smooth satin edge.
Our job was to sort and pick
through one bundle each day.
To sort and pick
through one history each day.

The tall girl fetched a bundle
and laid it before me.
When I untied the knot,
the blue quilt quickly revealed
the small parts of people's lives.

I pictured soldiers
walking through apartments of displaced Jews,
boisterous, haughty,
their boots loud and careless
in the gloom of ghosts.
Laughter as they laid a blanket
or tablecloth on the floor
and dumped the contents
of drawers from dressing table and bureau,
desk and sewing-room cabinet,

toeing back with booted foot
anything that rolled away.
Tying the corners
lugging the bundles
with the disregard of a fruit merchant
taking out the trash
to the truck in the street.
To come here.

Embarrassed,
ashamed
to peek
through cracks in a shutter
at the pieces of lives
spread before me.
Piles for cloth and thread.
Cotton and silk put aside.
Pins and needles and scissors.
A thimble worn smooth.
A manicure set with dull ivory handles.
A tortoiseshell hand mirror.
Eyeglasses.
A small yellowed envelope

with *Hana* written on the front
in a graceful hand.
Inside, a lock of raven hair.

Worst were the photographs.
Generations of families looking at me.
Nameless men and women.
Children, elders.
(Would I see someone I knew?
The thought was a snake
in my stomach.)
Bound by blood
now held together in albums
or in small piles tied with ribbon.

The work was easy, I was told.
But soon defeated by my wretched sadness
I chose the absolution of the cold
where I stacked wood
or lugged stone
until my fingers bled.

SS Lieutenant Theodor Lang

Because of the meddlesome king of Denmark
we were forced
to allow
Red Cross inspectors to visit our town.
We had months to prepare
our show, a charade
to show them that there was no truth
to the pesky rumors about how
we treated our Jews.

Before we could initiate our beautification program
we needed to solve overcrowding.
We needed cattle cars
locomotives to rid the town of 17,000 Jews
mostly the sick and old.
They fought
at the sight of the cattle cars.

But they went.
It was not easy moving so many infirmed
but our system worked flawlessly.

With the population controlled,
we opened shops
where Jews could buy used clothes,
luggage, trinkets,
mostly things they had relinquished
when they arrived.
We opened a splendid café
on the main square,
a place for Jews to sit and chat
to be noticed by the inspectors.

To show the world
that we are not heartless,
the numbers and letters of the streets
were changed to names.
Ghetto Theresienstadt
seemed harsh,
so it became *Jüdisches Ansiedlung*.

The town square needed attention.
It was fenced from the population
except for the thousand Jews
who worked in a large white tent
making boxes.
We closed the factory
took down the tent
removed the fence,
replaced them with grass,
flowers with colorful blossoms
(don't ask me their names).
We erected a music pavilion,
a playground for Jew children,
allowed all Jews to enjoy
the four parks in our town.
Would we do these things
if we were not thinking of the Jews?

We did more for the Jews.
We turned a hall that had been filled
with encephalitic Jews—
gone on the first transport—
into a social club
for music recitals and lectures.

We gave the Jews a library.
A synagogue.
Even a columbarium
to store the ashes
of the Jews who'd died in our town.
Quite compassionate,
I would say.

To make certain the world knew
how we treated Jews
we permitted the Jew children
to perform *Brundibár,*
a frothy fairy tale
that delighted the visitors.

The inspectors
were in our town for a short time,
only long enough to see
what we wanted them to see.
No more.
They saw enough
to know that we were treating the Jews
in a civilized and humane manner.

We waited a few months
to resume the transports.
The town was getting crowded
and the ovens of Auschwitz waited.

Eliska Schorr / 25565

I am a watcher,
sitting with those about to die.
There are so many to watch;
some leave unnoticed.
Today I sit with Frieda
but not for long.
I will stay with her
until it is time to summon the hearse.

Her eyes are open
but she cannot see,
her mouth a slit
although she cannot speak.
A filthy sheet pulled to her chin
cannot mask the sour stench
of her soiled bedding.

Frieda came to this place
with a moon face
jolly eyes
and folds of fat,
her housedress
a bedsheet billowing on the wash line.
Her husband was transported
at the end of the first spring.
I recall the new leaves,
children playing with a black cat.
The door of the cattle car slammed
shut.
She wept.
Eyes watched
through the slats.
Hands reached for other hands.

Typhus took her daughter
on a winter night
with a ghost of a moon.

So Frieda comes to this.
Too weak to welcome death,
she leaves that to me.

I will stay with her
until it is time
to close her eyelids
wrap the wretched sheet around her bones.
I will stay with her
and wait for the hearse.

Otto Beck

The Jews are taking over
the town.
Who invited them?
Not I.
They swarm down the street
like locusts
to infest the town.
Friends moved away.
Shops closed.
The tavern.
I nearly lost
my apartment,
but I answered the call
to become a *strażnik*.
I like keeping the peace.
It is a noble calling.

The Jews are weak.
They let the soldiers push them around.
I would never permit that,
not without throwing some punches.
That I know.

I keep the peace,
make sure the Jews know their place.
When I growl, they cower.
Occasionally, there is one
who doesn't look down fast enough
or step aside
when I pass.
That earns a shove or a slap.

There are rumors, of course,
but what is that to me?
I do my job here
in Terezín
keeping the peace.

Mother marked each day
on a loaf of bread
that had to last
one week

Izak Posselberg / 43445

My beloved,
I long
to know
the beat of your heart
again
and fill each
brief
silence
with a kiss
until
curved together
we sleep.

Nicolas was adorable
in our opera
as Brundibár
complete with false mustache.
He sang—
such a voice!—
marched around the stage
beaming
aglow with pride.
Applause washed over him
over all of us.
He *was* Brundibár.

His star flashed for sixteen days
until his number was called.

His mother's, too.

And his sister's.

As Nicolas clattered toward death

we found a new Brundibár.

I was a cat
with cat freedom
even if for only thirty minutes
even if I spoke but two lines
before it was back to the barracks
overcrowded with
the stink of bodies
the stink of fear
the stink of death.
But for those few minutes
I was free as any cat.

I know you are hungry, too,
little sparrow,
but I need more

more than crumbs
to fill my belly.

My friends are lost.

Sarah wanted to marry a rich doctor
who would buy her flowers
and chocolates
and otherwise pamper her shamelessly
until her dying day.
Transport 5712.

Zofia and I slept outside whenever
it was allowed
holding hands
counting stars
until we fell asleep.
Transport 2174.

Anna, always serious,
gave me the rag doll
her mama had made.
"You need it," she said.
"I'm leaving."
Transport 1753.

Olga stopped eating
the day after her parents died of typhus.
Just stopped
and became a sacred sack of sticks
that I bore in my arms
to the hearse.

Kamila, with emerald eyes,
so happy,
happy she wasn't going
to be separated from her parents.
Transport 6714.

Dorcas adored her uncle
followed him
from a fourth-floor window
to the cobbled courtyard.

Jolanta left in winter.
I watched her footprints
fill with snow.
Transport 1175.

I am lost.
I will leave my rag doll.
Transport 9177.

Morning moon,
crescent,
centered
in the window
beyond bare branches.
The hearse, too, is silent.

Wilfried Becker / 34507

When Otto's number was called,
Eva wept.
She would go with him.
Insisted.
They would have one more night
together.
She traded half a loaf of bread
for two hours
in a *kumbal* with a curtain.
Otto asked if I would play
my violin.
"I would be honored, my friend."
"Can you play Johann Strauss?"
I smiled. "I am German, am I not?"

So it was that on a frigid night
I played waltzes for them.

"The Blue Danube"
"Where the Lemons Bloom"
"Youthful Dreams"
all played softly
notes like stars.

When they pulled back the curtain
and nodded to me,
I bowed
and played a final waltz.

Franz Keller

I am honored, *Herr General,*
that you have come to see
our crematorium,
the newest in the protectorate.

Let me show you how it works.
This body wrapped in sheets
will not object
to being part of our demonstration.
He—although in truth we cannot tell,
nor care if it be she or he—
is placed on the iron trolley
and slid into the furnace—
headfirst to help with drainage.
The trolley dumps the body—see?—
then is retrieved and readied for another.

You hear that roar?
The flame port starts
and soon the temperature
will reach between one thousand
and twelve thousand degrees,
using six to nine liters of oil
to maintain a suitable temperature
until eighty percent of the body
has been devoured.

How does the body burn, you ask?
Outside to inside
layer by layer
dehydration
ignition
even though we are mostly water.
Heat dries the skin,
which ignites;
muscle and fat dry out,
ignite;
after muscle and fat,
organs flare and burn.

No, the stomach does not explode.
Nor the head.
Those are merely myths, sir,
although the cranium may split like a melon
and the brains drain out.
That I have seen several times.

You are all very busy, I know,
so you need not remain until
the process is complete.
That could take two hours for a man,
less for a woman.

Yes, *Herr General*, the process is slow.
More ovens would make quicker work of it.
Yes, we could burn two bodies at once.
I will make a note, *Herr General*.

The bones are raked
to the center of the chamber.
When they are finally ash
they are dumped to the lower chamber
sifted
left to cool

then scooped into paper urns.
Yes, those boxes you see
stacked against the wall.
Finally, the urns are taken
to the columbarium,
which, I am told, used to be a brewery.
True, *Herr General,*
we all must sacrifice.

Sofie Pearl / 10477

Transport 7131,
Samuel was told.
Sounded benign,
like a trolley to Wenceslas Square
soft seat, conversations,
a bell to signal a stop.
But this was different.
A string of cattle cars
penned-in desperation
locomotive black as death
whistle a hysterical scream.
This was a death train.
We'd heard the stories,
knew the names:
Ravensbrück
Buchenwald
Dachau.

Transport 7131:
Auschwitz.

The morning the men lined up,
birds sang
sitting on a tidy white fence
in front of the *Kommandant*'s house.
After twenty years together
I waited with Samuel.
We said nothing.
There were too many words to say.
A delirious man standing with his family
was clubbed by the guards, dragged off,
his head snapping on the cobbles,
his arms trailing
like the wake of a ship.

At the *Schleuse*
Samuel looked down at me.
His words slurred with sadness.
"So, our love comes to this."
I could only whisper,
"It is our lives that come to this."
I folded his hands in mine

four hands squeezed in prayer.
"Our love continues in me, in you."

Each time a rail car door slammed
it was a kick in my heart,
until the door to Samuel's car slammed
(was it louder than the others?)
nearly bringing me to my knees.
But I stood
alone
as darkness joined me.

Corporal Krebs, whose face seemed out of place
among bullies and thugs,
said softly, "You must leave, *Fräulein*."
"Or what?
You will club me?
Shoot me in my heart?"
"*Bitte, Fräulein.*"

The train whistle's wail grew
louder
louder,
in grief

I was sure.

How odd.

Even as Samuel moved away from me
the wail grew louder.

"You must be silent, *Fräulein.*"
Only then did I recognize
the wail of my empty heart.

Blue sky
beyond
barbed wire.

I wish I were
sky.

Afterword

In the fall of 1941, the Nazis turned Terezín, Czechoslovakia, a fortress town on the banks of the Ohre River, into a collection and transport camp for Jews. After displacing all the residents, the Nazis changed its name to Ghetto Theresienstadt. The first transport from Prague arrived on November 11, 1941, and consisted of 324 men—carpenters, painters, laborers—whose job was to ready the town for the thousands of Jews who would be arriving.

What set Terezín apart from Nazi death camps was the nature of many of its inmates. Terezín became "home" for many of the Jewish intellectuals and artists of Prague. As a result, it became a prison in which the arts were tolerated, then encouraged as a Nazi propaganda tool. Classical music and opera performances were commonplace, despite the horrors and cruelty of captivity. Lectures were delivered in attics and basements of the barracks. Most such activities were allowed by the Nazis, who saw these artistic events as proof to the world that they were treating the Jews humanely and allowing their culture to flourish. The reality of the situation was, of course, quite the opposite. Musicians who performed beautifully one night were packed into cattle cars the next, transported to the gas chambers.

By the time the Russian army liberated Terezín on April 20, 1945, nearly 140,000 European Jews had passed through the camp. About 35,000 never left Terezín, victims of disease, starvation, and brutality. Another 87,000 were transported to other concentration camps, such as Auschwitz, where all but a small number perished.

Author's Note

Although the poems in this collection are based on historical events and facts, most of the characters that appear in the poems are fictional. Some are composites based on my research. Others are totally invented. One exception is "Valtr Eisinger/11956," a found poem taken from letters written by Eisinger, which I located in *We Are Children Just the Same.* Valtr Eisinger was shot at Buchenwald on January 15, 1945.

Beyond that, my writing was informed by my research. "Izak Posselberg/43445," for example, is a poem of twenty-five words that I wrote after I discovered that in the early months of the ghetto, inmates were allowed to send postcards to loved ones, as long as they were no longer than twenty-five words. While some of the events described in my poems actually happened—the census in "Ruth Posner/14161" and the Red Cross inspection in "SS Lieutenant Theodor Lang," for example—the characters, their thoughts, and their conversations are products of my imagination.

The composers that I mention in "Anna Teller/12727"—Viktor Ullmann, Hans Krása, Pavel Haas, and Gideon Klein—were inmates at Terezín before being transported to their deaths in Nazi gas chambers.

In addition to the print and Internet sources that I consulted, I visited Terezín and its memorial and museums on April 26, 2008.

I chose *Requiem* as the title of this collection because I saw many of the poems in it as solemn songs to the memory of the people who died within the walls of Theresienstadt.

Selected Sources

BOOKS

Auerbacher, Inge. *I Am a Star: Child of the Holocaust*. New York: Prentice-Hall, 1986.

Friedman, Saul S., ed. *The Terezin Diary of Gonda Redlich*. Lexington, KY: University Press of Kentucky, 1992.

Friesová, Jana Renée. *Fortress of My Youth: Memoir of a Terezín Survivor*. Madison, WI: University of Wisconsin Press, 2002.

Green, Gerald. *The Artists of Terezin*. New York: Hawthorn Books, 1978.

Krizkova, Marie Ruth, et al., *We Are Children Just the Same*. Philadelphia: The Jewish Publication Society, 1995.

Kushner, Tony. *Brundibar*. New York: Michael Di Capua/Hyperion, 2003.

Roubickova, Eva. *We're Alive and Life Goes On*. New York: Henry Holt, 1998.

Rubin, Susan Goldman. *Fireflies in the Dark*. New York: Holiday House, 2000.

Schiff, Vera. *Theresienstadt: The Town the Nazis Gave to the Jews*. Toronto: Lugus, 1996.

Spies, Gerty. *My Years in Theresienstadt*. Amherst, NY: Prometheus Books, 1997.

Troller, Norbert. *Theresienstadt: Hitler's Gift to the Jews*. Chapel Hill, NC: University of North Carolina Press, 1991.

WEBSITES

Center for Holocaust & Genocide Studies, University of Minnesota
http://chgs.umn.edu/museum/memorials/terezin/

History of the Theresienstadt Ghetto
http://www.scrapbookpages.com/CzechRepublic/
Theresienstadt/TheresienstadtGhetto/History/index.html

Jewish Virtual Library
http://www.jewishvirtuallibrary.org/jsource/Holocaust/
terezintoc.html

The Terezín Memorial
http://www.pruvodce.com/terezin/index_en.php3

The Dayton Holocaust Resource Center
http://daytonholocaust.org

The United States Holocaust Memorial Museum
http://www.ushmm.org/

DVDs

Holocaust: Theresienstadt. Arts Magic, 2005.

A Town Marked by Tragedy: Chapters from Terezín's History. Terezín Memorial/Studio Grant, 2006.

Foreign Words and Phrases

Schleuse (German) — sluice or entryway
strażnik (Czech) — guard or warden
Judisches Ansiedlung (German) — Jewish settlement
kumbál (Czech) — alcove or closet

Art Credits

p. viii: "Entering the Camp" by Fritz Lederer, 1946; reprinted courtesy of Eli Lev.

p. 5: "Registration for a Transport" by Karel Fleischmann, reprinted by permission of the Jewish Museum in Prague and the Ministry of Culture.

p. 11: "Two Old Men" by Karel Fleischmann, reprinted by permission of the Jewish Museum in Prague and the Ministry of Culture.

pp. 16–17: "Prayer in the Attic" by Ferdinand Bloch, reprinted by permission of the Jewish Museum in Prague and the Ministry of Culture.

p. 32: "A View of Terezín" by Bedrich Fritta copyright by Tomáš Fritta-Haas, on permanent loan to the Jewish Museum Berlin; reprinted by permission of Tomáš Fritta-Haas.